DOYLE AND FOSSEY, SCIENCE DETECTIVES

The Case of the Barfy Birthday

(and Other Super-Scientific Cases)

MICHELE TORREY

ILLUSTRATED BY
BARBARA JOHANSEN NEWMAN

STERLING CHILDREN'S BOOKS
New York

To Mom & Dad,
my handy-dandy references
for inspiration, answers, and hugs
M. T.

For the editor extraordinaire,
Meredith Mundy—
truly a pleasure to work with and a master
at the fine art of nurturing and nudging
B. J. N.

STERLING CHILDREN'S BOOKS
New York

An Imprint of Sterling Publishing
387 Park Avenue South
New York, NY 10016

STERLING CHILDREN'S BOOKS and the distinctive Sterling Children's Books logo
are trademarks of Sterling Publishing Co., Inc.

Text © 2003, 2009 by Michele Torrey
Illustrations © 2003, 2009 Barbara Johansen Newman

ISBN 978-1-4027-4964-3

Library of Congress Cataloging-in-Publication Data Available

Distributed in Canada by Sterling Publishing
c/o Canadian Manda Group, 165 Dufferin Street
Toronto, Ontario, Canada M6K 3H6
Distributed in the United Kingdom by GMC Distribution Services
Castle Place, 166 High Street, Lewes, East Sussex, England BN7 1XU
Distributed in Australia by Capricorn Link (Australia) Pty. Ltd.
P.O. Box 704, Windsor, NSW 2756, Australia

For information about custom editions, special sales,
and premium and corporate purchases, please contact Sterling Special Sales
at 800-805-5489 or specialsales@sterlingpublishing.com.
Manufactured in the United States of America
Lot #:
2 4 6 8 10 9 7 5 3
11/11
This book originally published in hardcover by Dutton Children's Books in 2003

www.sterlingpublishing.com/kids

CONTENTS

CHAPTER ONE
Situation Critical

It was a perfectly lazy Sunday afternoon in the small town of Mossy Lake. Just the sort of day for a barbecue or a stroll in the park.

Unless you happened to be Drake Doyle.

Tucked away in his attic lab, surrounded by test tubes, Drake was up to his ears in experiments. Sometimes he said, "Aha!" if things went especially well. Or sometimes, if things didn't go precisely so, he exclaimed, "Great Scott!" or even "Egads!"

Drake's cinnamon-colored hair stuck straight up, as if he'd seen a ghost. (Which he had, but that's another story.) He looked quite spiffy in his lab coat, because it had his name on it. A pencil stuck out from behind his ear.

1

Drake punched numbers into his calculator and peered at the results. He scribbled in his lab notebook:

Incredible, but true.
Numbers crunch perfectly.
Analysis a success.

But before he could call his partner, Nell Fossey, and tell her about his perfectly crunching numbers, the phone rang.

"Doyle and Fossey," he answered.

You see, Drake never answered his phone in any other way. The reason was simple. Drake was a professional. In fact, he and Nell were the most professional amateur science detective team in the fifth grade. Whenever there was a nasty case to solve (or even a not-so-nasty case), Drake and Nell were the ones to call. Already they'd solved many cases involving ghosts, monsters, and kidnapped parrots, to name a few. Their business cards read:

Doyle and Fossey:
Science Detectives
call us. anytime. 555-7822

"Detective Doyle?" said the caller.

Drake recognized Zoe Jackson's voice. Zoe was in Drake and Nell's class. Just yesterday, they had attended a birthday party for her and her twin sister, Chloe. Zoe was a nice girl, and a health nut besides. She jogged to school, drank her protein lunch, and ran an exercise program called "Fabulous Fitness for Flabby Folks" on rainy days during recess.

"Oh, hi, Zoe. What seems to be the problem?"

"Can you and Nell hurry to the emergency room at Mossy Lake Hospital?" asked Zoe.

Drake nearly dropped the phone. The hospital! Great Scott! This had to be critical! Drake kept his voice calm. "You can count on us, Ms. Jackson. We'll be there. ASAP."

He wasted no time before calling Nell. "I'll pick you up, ASAP. Situation critical."

"Check."

Click.

Drake sprang to his feet, grabbed some essential equipment, and hurried down the attic stairs. "Dad! Dad!"

"What! What!" Mr. Sam Doyle met him at the bottom of the steps, looking very worried.

"Situation critical! Nell and I need a ride to the ER, ASAP!"

"Oh. Whew! For a second there, I thought you'd blown up the lab."

Together they hurried out to the car. Soon they were racing toward Nell's house. You see, no one could speed around corners quite like Mr. Doyle. Plus, he owned a science equipment and supply company. If Drake needed anything for his lab, he only had to ask. Computers, beakers, lab coats with their names on them, test tubes—it didn't matter so long as Drake didn't blow up the lab. (He'd only blown up the lab three times so far, but who's counting?)

They screeched to a stop in front of Nell's house. She was waiting for them on the sidewalk and looked ready to tackle anything. Hair the color of coffee was pulled into a tight ponytail, guaranteed to stay out of the way while speeding around corners. She slid into the backseat, buckled her seat belt, and gripped the armrest. "Step on it, Mr. Doyle."

"Check."

Va-room!

They turned here. They turned there. Meanwhile, Drake told Nell about his phone conversation with Zoe. Finally, they screeched to a stop in front of the hospital. *Screech!*

And off they rushed. (Unfortunately, Drake didn't see the glass doors and ran right into them with a *bonk!* Nell had to rub his head until he stopped looking cross-eyed.)

Nell opened the door for Drake, and they hurried inside. The emergency room was packed. Nurses hollered, "Code Purple!" Doctors said, "This won't hurt a bit." Grandmas moaned, "Ohhh." Grandpas groaned, "Bleh." Babies wailed, "Wah!" Parents cried, "Get me outta here!"

And in the middle of all that hubbub, someone grabbed Nell's arm. It was Zoe. She was wearing sunglasses and a trench coat. "Shh," she whispered. "This way." She led them behind a big leafy plant. "No one can see us here."

Drake and Nell exchanged glances. "What seems to be the trouble, Ms. Jackson?" asked Drake. "Why the secrecy?"

"It's my twin sister, Chloe." Zoe parted the plant and pointed across the lobby. Indeed, there sat Chloe. Both Drake and Nell gasped because, you see, Chloe didn't look like she usually did. Normally Chloe was happy and smiling. Today, however, she looked terribly, terribly sick.

And while they watched, Chloe bent over a basin on her lap and . . . well . . . barfed. (No

delicate way to explain it, really, except to just say it like it is.)

"Eew," said Zoe.

"Ugh," said Nell.

"Oh dear," said Drake.

Zoe sighed. "She's been doing that all day. At this rate, she'll turn inside out before the doctors even call her name. Poor, poor Chloe!"

Nell flipped open her lab notebook and whipped a pencil out from behind her ear. "Why don't you take it from the top, Ms. Jackson."

Zoe nodded. She cleared her throat. She paced just a wee bit. (Pacing is limited behind big, leafy plants.) "You see . . ."

"Yes?" asked Drake, his pencil poised over his notebook.

Zoe adjusted her sunglasses. She paced a bit more. "You see . . ."

"Yes?" asked Nell, tapping her foot.

Finally Zoe stopped. She peered over her sunglasses and looked them square in the eye. "I think I poisoned my sister."

CHAPTER TWO

Barfy Business

"*Poisoned your sister?*" Drake and Nell said together.

"Shh! Lower your voices," said Zoe. "I'm looking at life in prison here. Maybe only ten years, if I'm lucky."

"But how—" started Drake.

"But why—" started Nell.

"Believe me, it was an accident. This morning Chloe said she didn't have any energy, so I fixed her a health shake."

"And what was in this health shake?" asked Nell.

"Let me see . . . peanuts, milk, fish oil, carrot juice, spinach, garlic, oranges, anchovies, and vanilla ice cream—nonfat, of course. Just the thing for boosting energy."

8

"And she drank it?" asked Drake, shuddering at the thought.

Zoe nodded. "Every drop. And that's when it all ... you know ... started. Oh, poor, poor Chloe!"

"Indeed," murmured Drake, jotting everything down.

"Quick question, Ms. Jackson," said Nell, making a few final notes. "What exactly is it you want us to do?"

Drake looked at his partner, stunned. It was a brilliant question and he was surprised he hadn't thought of it, too.

"I want you to make an antidote to counteract the poison." Zoe stopped pacing and stuck her hands in her trench-coat pockets. "You're my last chance between freedom and prison. You're my last chance to save Chloe. Unless, of course, I call Frisco."

Frisco! Drake and Nell exchanged horrified looks. James Frisco was also in their fifth-grade class at school. Like Doyle and Fossey, Frisco was a scientist, but that's where the resemblance ended. You see, Frisco enjoyed it when beakers bubbled over. Frisco grinned when things exploded. Frisco laughed out loud while pouring dangerous chemicals down the drain.

Frisco's business cards read:

```
FRISCO
b̶a̶d̶ mad scientist
(Better than Doyle and Fossey)
Call me. Day or night. 555-6190
```

Drake could never let Zoe call Frisco! If Zoe called Frisco, he'd likely fill a bottle with dishwater, call it an antidote, and charge her five bucks plus tax and a tip. Who knows what would happen to Chloe without a proper antidote! The thought was too terrible to imagine!

"Never fear, Ms. Jackson, we'll take the case," said Drake.

"Say," said Nell, peering through the plant to where Chloe was sitting. "Isn't that your mother sitting beside Chloe?"

"Yes," answered Zoe, "what about her?"

"She looks sick, too."

Drake agreed. Mrs. Jackson was the color of mashed peas, with perhaps a splotch of spinach green here and there.

Zoe nodded. "Yes, but she didn't drink any health shake, so there's no worry there."

"And isn't that Lilly Crump sitting two seats away from Mrs. Jackson?" asked Nell.

Drake pushed up his glasses. Egads! Nell was right again! Just like Chloe and Chloe's mother, Lilly was barfing into a basin!

"Hmm," said Nell, "the last time we saw Lilly was yesterday at the birthday party."

"I have a hunch," said Drake, his mind working furiously.

"Ditto," said Nell.

They pulled on surgical gloves.

Snap! Snap!

They marched across the waiting room.

"Afternoon, Chloe," said Drake, patting her on the shoulder.

"Ooooooh, help me," she moaned.

"Sorry you're not feeling well," said Drake.

Nell patted her other shoulder. "Do you mind if we examine you? Perhaps we can help."

"Anything," said Chloe weakly.

"Just try to relax," said Nell. "This will be over in a jiffy."

Mrs. Jackson moved over a couple of seats to make room for them. "Do whatever you need to do," she said.

"Check," replied Drake and Nell. They took

11

Chloe's pulse. They took her temperature. They had her say "Aaaaah." They asked her and her mother a few questions. Then, just as Drake was pondering, Chloe leaned over, missed the basin, and . . . well . . .

Barf! . . .

Splat! . . .

. . . all over Drake's shoes. (It was one of those curious scientific moments when, just for a second or two, Drake wished he'd picked a different career.)

Chloe groaned. "Sorry."

But Drake was a professional. Even when splattered with barf. "No problem. Now, if you'll excuse us."

"Indeed," said Nell with a nod. "Get well soon."

And after questioning Lilly, plus a quick trip to the restroom for barf removal, both Drake and Nell were ready for action.

"There's no time to lose!" cried Nell. "Back to the lab for analysis!"

"And a shower . . ." added Drake.

CHAPTER THREE

In the Bag

Drake pulled a book off the shelf and sat next to Nell at the lab table.

He flipped through the pages until he found the right section: "Situation Critical: What to Do When You've Given Your Twin Sister a Health Drink and She Barfs and Barfs and Barfs." After Drake read the section aloud, they discussed their observations. (Good scientists always discuss their observations.)

Finally, Drake said, "I have developed a hypothesis." (A hypothesis, as every good scientist knows, is a scientist's best guess as to what is happening.)

"Couldn't have said it better myself, Detective Doyle," said Nell with a nod after Drake had explained his idea. "Let's test it."

And so, they got to work. In this case, it was detective work. Telephone detective work, to be precise. They were into their fifth phone call when Drake's mother, Kate Doyle, poked her head around the door. "Do you two brilliant scientists want anything to eat or drink? Hot chocolate, perhaps? Deviled eggs? A muffin or two?"

"Muffins," said Drake. "Blueberry. Hold the hot chocolate."

"Coffee," said Nell. "Decaf. Black. And two deviled eggs. No, make it three." (In case you weren't up on the latest in the scientific world, real scientists don't drink hot chocolate. Ditto for real detectives. They prefer coffee. Decaf. Black. With muffins upon occasion. And don't forget the deviled eggs.)

"No problemo," replied Mrs. Doyle. Just as Drake's dad was great for science equipment and driving fast, Drake's mom was fabulous for food and drink. In fact, Mrs. Doyle owned her own company: Kate Doyle's Fab Foods.

One phone call and one chart later, Mrs. Doyle was back with hot coffee (decaf, black), muffins (blueberry), and eggs (deviled).

"Now eat those eggs right away," said Mrs. Doyle. "Don't let them get warm, because you know what can happen . . ." And she warned them about the dangers that could lurk in food kept out of the fridge for too long.

"Thanks for the hot tip, Mom," said Drake.

"And thanks for the fab food," said Nell, before popping a deviled egg into her mouth.

After Mrs. Doyle left, Drake and Nell returned to making phone calls and drawing charts.

The phone calls sounded a lot alike.

"Hello?" the person would answer, usually in a very weak or wobbly sort of voice. Then Drake or Nell would ask a few questions about yesterday's birthday party. Then they'd have to wait while . . . *barf!* . . .

Then, Drake or Nell would say, "Get to the ER, ASAP. Situation critical."

After each phone call, Drake and Nell filled in more details on the master chart. (Details like who was sick, who ate a hamburger, who took a refreshing dip in the pool, and so forth.)

Finally, three muffins and two and a half cups of decaf later, Nell announced, "We have our answer! Quick! Back to the hospital!"

While Mr. Doyle's car screeched around this corner and that corner, Nell called her mom, Professor Ann Fossey, on Mr. Doyle's cell phone. "I'll be home in an hour, maybe less. The Case of the Barfy Birthday is in the bag," replied Nell.

"That's nice, honey. I hope you're remembering to wash your hands frequently." Now, this might seem like an odd thing for a parent to say, but for Professor Fossey it was perfectly normal. Professor Fossey was a scientist herself. She taught wildlife biology at Mossy Lake University, and so she knew all about good laboratory technique and washing your hands.

"Don't worry, Mom. It's in the bag."

When they arrived, the ER was very crowded. Sitting with Chloe, Mrs. Jackson, and Lilly were all of the people Drake and Nell had phoned.

Zoe dashed up and pulled Drake and Nell behind the potted plant. "Quick! The antidote!"

Drake and Nell glanced at each other. "We apologize, Ms. Jackson," Drake said gravely, "but there is no antidote."

There followed a moment of stunned silence (if you ignored the general hubbub). Then Zoe paced, talking aloud. "I wonder if there's still time to hire Frisco. Or jog to the Mexican border."

"Relax, Zoe," said Nell. "No antidote is needed."

Zoe looked confused. "What do you mean?"

"You didn't poison your sister," said Drake.

Zoe's mouth dropped open.

"Allow Scientist Nell to explain," added Drake.

Now it was Nell's turn to pace behind the plant. "Imagine yourself lying in bed. You roll over just as your alarm clock rings. Now, did your alarm clock go off *because* you rolled over? Of course not. They merely happened at the same time."

Zoe glanced at her watch. "I really should be getting to the Mexican border."

"You see, Ms. Jackson," Nell continued, "just because two things appear to be related does not mean that they are. You thought you poisoned your sister because she barfed when she drank the health shake. The truth is, she was already sick, and your health shake just tasted nasty."

"Are you sure?" asked Zoe. "That's good, I guess. But what made her sick?"

"Excellent question," said Nell.

Drake pushed up his glasses. "We first became suspicious when we observed that your mother was also sick. And, of course, there was Lilly Crump, green as a guppy. Coincidence? Maybe. To find out, we did a little investigating."

"We discovered that all three had become sick

at the same time," said Nell. "And all three were at your birthday party yesterday."

"Very suspicious indeed," said Drake.

"So you think something at the party made them sick?" asked Zoe.

Drake nodded. "Precisely. We called everyone who attended the party. We wanted to know where they sat, what they ate, and so on."

"I don't understand," said Zoe.

"You soon will. Chart, please!" ordered Nell.

Drake unrolled a chart. Nell whipped out her wooden pointer and whapped the chart. "Observe. Out of the eighteen people who attended the party, eleven became sick. You will notice that everyone who became sick had one thing in common. They all ate the chicken salad. Those who didn't eat the chicken salad didn't get sick."

Zoe frowned. "I still don't get it. Why would chicken salad make people sick?"

"Bacteria," said Nell.

"Bacteria?" asked Zoe.

"Germs, if I may be so blunt," said Drake. "Bacteria, or germs, are tiny organisms that live everywhere. They can make people sick." Drake rolled up the chart and began to pace. "You will recall that yesterday was rather warm."

CAKE   PIÑATA

NAME	SICK?	ATE CAKE	SWUNG AT PIÑATA	ATE CHICKEN SALAD	DIP IN POOL	DRANK PUNCH	ATE HAMBURGER	PUNCH
ZOE	N	Y	Y	N	Y	Y	Y	
CHLOE	Y	Y	N	N	Y	Y	Y	
MRS. JACKSON	Y	N	N	Y	N	N	N	
DRAKE	N	N	Y	Y	N	Y	Y	
NELL	N	N	N	Y	Y	Y	Y	
LILY	Y	Y	Y	Y (3X)	Y (RX)	Y (8X)	Y (6X)	
BALDWIN	Y	Y	Y	Y	Y	Y	N	
SLOANE	Y	Y	Y	Y	Y	Y	N	

HAMBURGER

SALAD
CHICKEN

"Hot, in fact," added Nell. "Bacteria love to grow where it's warm."

"After a few hours of sitting in the hot sun," said Drake, "the bacteria multiplied and multiplied until the chicken salad was loaded with them. One bite would have made anyone sick."

"So I *did* poison everyone!" Zoe moaned. "I'll get life in prison for sure!"

"It's called food poisoning," said Drake. "Easily prevented by keeping hot food hot and cold food cold. Never warm. Unless you eat it right away. And, of course, everyone knows to wash their hands frequently. Preparing food with dirty hands is the leading cause of food poisoning."

After giving Zoe a few more important food-serving tips, they spied the doctor talking with Mrs. Jackson. Drake and Nell hurried over.

"So glad you're here," Drake and Nell said to the doctor. They shook her hand. They quickly explained the problem, raising their voices to be heard over the chorus of barfs. They gave her the chart, plus their business card.

"Fine work, Doyle and Fossey," said the doctor. "You've saved us a lot of trouble. As busy as we are today, I don't know if we'd have made the connection. We'll test the chicken salad for bacteria, and meanwhile start the appropriate treatment. Your friends should feel much better in a day or two. Of course we'll notify the proper authorities."

"The authorities!" cried Zoe. "Oh my gosh, I'm going to prison over chicken salad!" And she crumpled on the floor in a heap of trench coat.

The doctor looked confused. "Uh—no, actually, I was talking about the public health authorities. They like to know about food-poisoning outbreaks. Anyway, job well done, Doyle and Fossey. I'll take it from here."

That evening before dinner, Drake wrote in his lab notebook:

Case of the Barfy Birthday Solved. Never underestimate bacteria. Received Zoe's recipe for health shake. (YUCK. MUST SHRED RECIPE BEFORE MOM FINDS IT.)
Paid in full. (I THINK.)

CHAPTER FOUR
A Terrible Tragedy

It was a rather warm Saturday morning and, once again, Drake was busy in his laboratory. On this particular occasion, he carefully swabbed his nose. (On the inside, to be scientifically precise.) Then, lifting the lid of the petri dish, he rubbed the swab over a jellylike substance.

"There," he said with satisfaction, closing the lid. He put the petri dish in the incubator, washed his hands, and scribbled in his lab notebook:

> Goober extraction complete.
> Bacteria should grow quite nicely.
> Check in 24 hours.

Just then, Mrs. Doyle popped her head around the door. "Dr. Livingston is here to see you."

"Send him in," replied Drake.

Dr. Livingston trotted in. Drake scratched behind Dr. Livingston's ears and said, "Good boy." Then Drake withdrew a note from the pouch that hung around Dr. Livingston's neck.

"Y5X6.Y4X3.Y3X2.Y2X6.Y4X5.Y3X2.Y2X5.Y1X6. Y3X4.Y5X6.Y3X5.Y5X3.Y1X5.Y3X4 . . ." began the note. (Of course, to anyone else, it would look like gibberish. But Drake was a detective, and a fine detective at that. And, like all fine detectives everywhere, Drake was never without his code book.) Wasting no time, he whipped his pencil out from behind his ear and got to work. Soon he had the message decoded. It read:

> Detective Doyle,
> A terrible tragedy is at hand. Meet me at Nature Headquarters ASAP.
> Signed,
> Naturalist Nell

Drake pushed up his glasses. "A terrible tragedy is at hand!" he exclaimed. "We must hurry to Nature Headquarters!"

Woof!

• • •

Now, in case you think Nature Headquarters was nothing special, think again.

Enormous leaves dangled from papier-mâché trees. Chameleons changed colors. Hamsters took hamster naps. Ants scurried about. And fruit flies hatched. You see, Nature Headquarters was the code name for Nell's bedroom. Everything there had to do with nature. (This was only natural, as naturalists love nature.)

Drake moved a few vines. He wiped the steam off his glasses. Then he took a deep breath (of swamp gas, snake breath, and iguana toots), braced himself for the worst, and said, "Tragedy, you say?"

Nell sat at her desk, her mouth in a thin line. Beside her, under the lamp, was a small box. "A terrible tragedy," she replied.

"How so?"

"See for yourself." And she opened the box. Inside were six baby birds, nestled in a soft bed of grass. "There were eight hatchlings," said Nell, "but two of them have died already. These six are barely alive."

"Poor things," murmured Drake. "A terrible tragedy indeed."

Woof, said Dr. Livingston sadly.

"Where did you find them?" asked Drake.

"That's just it," said Nell, scratching her head. "Someone dumped them on my doorstep, box and all."

Drake gasped. "No note?"

"Nothing. My mom tripped over the box on her way to a wildlife convention. She wanted to help me, but had to hurry off and give a speech. She said to feed the hatchlings mushed-up fish and water, which I did."

"So now what?" asked Drake.

Nell got out her magnifying glass and examined the hatchlings. "From what I can tell, these are baby terns."

"Terns?" Drake pushed up his glasses.

Nell began to pace, moving vines and leaves. Dr. Livingston paced beside her. "You see, Detective Doyle, terns are related to gulls."

"Ah yes, Naturalist Nell," murmured Drake. "Gulls like to live by water, such as the ocean, or rivers, or lakes perhaps—"

"Correct," continued Nell. "So do terns. But this is no ordinary tern. No, indeed. The fact of the matter is, this species of tern is very rare."

"Rare, you say?" Drake took another peek into the box.

"When even one of these terns dies, it's a tragedy."

"What do you propose?" asked Drake.

Nell stopped her pacing and put her hands on her hips. "We must investigate Sand Island."

"Sand Island?"

"It's the nearest tern nesting site for a hundred miles."

Drake thought hard. "And you think something's gone wrong at the nesting site? Trouble perhaps?"

"Precisely," said Nell. "How else would someone have tern hatchlings? We must leave immediately. Doyle and Fossey to the rescue!"

Sand Island was, quite simply, made of sand. It was an attractive place . . . if you happened to be a tern. Really, there was nothing to be seen. No trees. No rocks. No shrubs. No nests.

And not a single tern.

Nell and Drake stepped out of the boat. (They'd left Dr. Livingston behind on the shore with Mr. Doyle. You see, while both Drake and Nell enjoyed Dr. Livingston's company immensely, they knew that dogs don't mix well with birds and hatchlings and nesting sites.)

Nell had brought the six hatchlings, hoping to reintroduce them to nests. But now she left the box in the boat and just shook her head. "The tragedy deepens."

"Indeed," said Drake.

"Where have all the terns gone?" she asked. "And why? Normally they dig a shallow depression in the sand for their nests, but I don't even see any of those."

"It's a mystery," said Drake. And he whipped a pencil out from behind his ear and opened his lab notebook, ready to investigate this most tragic mystery.

And so, like good detectives, they began to snoop.

"Hmm," murmured Nell as she examined some footprints with her magnifying glass.

"Aha," said Drake as he carefully took a sample of charred wood and placed it in a plastic bag for later analysis.

"Tragic," Nell said as she found a beer bottle here, a cigarette butt there, and used fireworks everywhere.

And just like that, their investigation was over. The answer was simple. Tragic, but simple.

CHAPTER FIVE
Barko's SuperMart

As soon as they finished strapping the boat onto the car, they climbed in and told Mr. Doyle about the deepening tragedy.

"That's terrible," he said. "What's next?"

Now, normally, this is an excellent question. But on this particular day, knowing what they knew, it was a tragic question. Because there was no easy answer. Drake and Nell just looked at each other and sighed sadly.

"I don't know," Nell finally answered, gazing out the window. "This case has taken a turn for the worse."

Then, just as Mr. Doyle turned left on Main Street, Drake and Nell got what you might call a lucky break.

There, flying high in the sky, was an adult tern. "Oh my gosh!" cried Nell. "Follow that tern!"

"Roger that!" said Mr. Doyle.

"And step on it!" cried Drake.

"Check!" said Mr. Doyle. They peeled around this corner and that, up one street and down another, all the while following the tern. (Mr. Doyle, as you know by now, was quite handy for turning sharply, stepping on it, and peeling around corners.)

Finally, they screeched to a stop in front of Barko's SuperMart.

They gasped at what they saw. Hundreds of terns were nesting on the roof, flying around, and living the bird life. "We've found them," whispered Nell.

"Target acquired," said Drake.

"They must have nested on the roof because they couldn't live on Sand Island anymore," said Nell. "A flat gravel roof was the best they could find."

Drake and Nell and Dr. Livingston hopped out of the car. Nell had the box of hatchlings under her arm. Just then, a friend from class came running up to them, looking quite frantic. Her name was Willow Barko, and her father owned

Barko's SuperMart. Willow was a friendly girl, always passing out sale flyers. She knew all about merchandising and clipping coupons and how to choose a cart without squeaky wheels. "Did you get my note? Did you get my note?" cried Willow.

"What note?" asked Nell.

"The one I left with the box of baby birds, asking you to take care of them and telling you to come quickly!"

Drake frowned. "Must have blown away. No matter. The important thing is, we're here now. How can we be of assistance, Ms. Barko?"

"This way!" she cried, and off she ran.

Drake and Nell exchanged glances and then ran after her. Willow stopped outside the entrance and pointed up. "The poor little hatchlings keep falling off the roof. I gathered up all the live ones, but they need your help or more will fall. I don't know what else to do!"

"We'll need a ladder," Nell said simply.

And without further ado, they propped a ladder against the side of the building and climbed onto the roof. (Dr. Livingston waited patiently below, picking a nice spot in the shade.) Scrappy nests were everywhere, scraped together with dirt, debris, and gravel. In the nests were tiny brown eggs and fluffy hatchlings. Adult terns flew around, some of them with fish in their beaks. Squawks and cheeps and flurries and flutters filled the air.

"Hmm," said Nell, walking carefully. "Notice how the adults must leave to find food to feed their chicks? There's nothing to stop the chicks from tumbling over the edge while their parents are gone."

Drake nodded, loosening his collar. "Not only that, but it's quite toasty up here. And there's zero shade for the hatchlings."

"Excellent observation, Detective Doyle." And, after putting on some gloves, Nell took the hatchlings from the box and placed one chick in each of six nests. "The best thing is to put them back into nests that already have hatchlings," she told Willow. "The adult birds will adopt the babies and take much better care of them than we can."

"But how will we keep more babies from falling off the roof?" asked Willow.

"Excellent question, Ms. Barko," said Drake.

And after conferring with one another, Drake and Nell and Willow hatched a plan.

With help from the employees and from caring shoppers, they put their plan into action.

Working as a team, they carried supplies onto the roof. And under Drake and Nell's direction, they built a low mesh fence all the way around the roof edge. They worked all afternoon, taking only one little break for iced tea and doughnuts fresh from Barko's Bakery. Finally, they added concrete blocks here and there to provide a bit of shade for the hot little hatchlings.

"Just right," said Drake, quite satisfied. "Now the hatchlings can't fall off the roof, and they have a bit of shade besides."

By the time they climbed down, a small crowd had gathered, including a reporter from the *Mossy Lake Daily Word*. "Doyle and Fossey, what can you tell us about Barko's bird invasion? Are the hatchlings really underfoot?"

(Now, you might think that this would be a little unnerving, but remember, good scientists are always prepared. Even when the cameras are on them. And microphones are in their faces. And everyone's looking at them for answers. And not just any answers. The right answers.)

First Nell cleared her throat. Then she told the reporters about the terns, and how rare they were. She told them about how the hatchlings couldn't fall off the roof any longer because of the fence.

(Dr. Livingston made a few comments as well.)

Then Drake told them how he'd added a spot of shade here and there. "Furthermore, the terns normally nest at Sand Island. But not anymore."

"And why is that?" asked the reporter.

"Habitat destruction," answered Nell. *(Arf!)*

"Come again?"

"You see," Nell continued, "Sand Island is a very delicate habitat. But people have invaded it, throwing parties, having weenie roasts, letting their dogs run on it, and who knows what else. Very simply, the birds had to move out. Habitat destruction is the leading cause of wildlife extinction." *(Woof!)*

"Oh," said the reporter. "That's terrible. What can be done to help the terns of Sand Island?"

Nell and Drake looked straight at the camera. This was their moment.

"The first order of business," said Drake most seriously, "is to clean up our act."

"Namely," added Nell, "clean up Sand Island and make it a place where the terns will come back to. We can lure them back with decoys and recorded tern calls. It's worked elsewhere; it can work here, too. I'll get my mom, Professor Fossey, to help us." *(Ruff!)*

"And after this," finished Drake, "leave Sand Island for the birds."

"One more thing," said Nell, turning toward Willow. "Special thanks to Willow Barko for bringing this most terrible tragedy to our attention." *(Arf! Arf!)*

"And thanks to Doyle and Fossey for such a happy ending," said Willow into the microphone. Then she waved at the camera, smiled sweetly, and added, "Barko's. The place to shop till you drop. Where the doughnuts are fresh and the people are friendly."

All in all, it was a happy turn of events.

At home, Drake wrote in his lab notebook:

Mystery of the Orphaned
Hatchlings solved.
Had us worried there for a
while. Habitat destruction a
nasty habit. Will work to clean
up our act.
Received a baker's dozen of
Barko's donuts.
            Paid in full.

CHAPTER SIX

Snob
Club

Early one Saturday morning, just as Nell was collecting data on hamster naps and gerbil snoozes, the phone rang.

Always the professional, she answered after the first ring. "Doyle and Fossey."

"Oh my gosh, I'm, like, *so* glad you're there. We've just had a totally *awful* night."

"Awful?" asked Nell, putting aside her notebook. "Who is this? And who is *we?*"

"It's, like, Valerie Applegate, who else?"

"Oh, hi, Valerie." Valerie was in Nell and Drake's class. Valerie was the sort of girl who was always fashionably late. Valerie never scraped her knees. Or burped. Or broke a fingernail. Or accidentally wore mismatched socks. In other words,

38

Valerie was cool. Now, being cool was all right with Nell, but Valerie was also a snob. She had her own group of snobs, too. Usually snobs like Valerie didn't call scientists like Nell, so Nell knew this had to be important.

"What can I do for you, Ms. Applegate?" asked Nell.

Valerie paused and then spoke with a rush. "Last night, you know, I, like, had some friends over to spend the night in my tree house? And we were, like, totally *haunted*."

Nell frowned. "Haunted? What do you mean?"

"Like, *hello*, haven't you ever heard of a ghost?"

Nell's heart tumbled in her chest. A ghost! She'd had a ghost case before, and it was no laughing matter. "We'll be right over," Nell said firmly. "You can count on us."

As soon as she hung up, Nell phoned Drake. "Ghost haunting at Valerie Applegate's tree house. Meet me there ASAP. No laughing matter."

"Check."

Click.

Like most tree houses, Valerie's tree house was, well . . . in a tree. Nell and Drake stood looking up, notebooks open and pencils ready.

"Take it from the top, Ms. Applegate."

Valerie stood beside them chewing a big wad of Snob Gob Gum. "Anyway, like I said, me and my friends? We were having this totally rockin' slumber party. And, like, well . . ."

Nell was astonished when Valerie's voice began to shake. ". . . We were, like, sitting there talking, when a blast of cold air hit me on the back of my neck. I mean, I'm not just talking about cold air, I'm talking about *totally* frigid air." Valerie shivered. "My grandpa said, that's, like, how ghosts feel when they're close to you. You know, the frozen dead. Corpses from the grave and stuff like that."

Drake scribbled furiously for a moment. "Frozen corpses, you say? Tell me, Ms. Applegate, where was the cold air coming from?"

"That's the thing. I mean, it was, like, coming from all around us. One minute from here, one minute from there. Like, you know, the hair stood up on the back of my neck. It was so spooky we had to go inside."

"Mind if we take a look around?" asked Nell.

"Like, for sure." Valerie blew a Snob Gob bubble. *Pop!* "And hurry up, will you? I haven't got all day, you know." With that, she went back into her house and pulled the blinds closed.

Sticking their pencils behind their ears and

putting their notebooks in their backpacks, Drake and Nell climbed the wooden boards hammered into the tree trunk.

"Just an ordinary tree house," said Nell, looking around.

"Agreed." Drake rapped the walls. "A little old. Gaps in the walls. Roof probably leaks when it rains. No secret passageways, no hidden doorways—nothing out of the ordinary." He drew a sketch and a graph, just in case. (Scientists never know what might come in handy later.)

Meanwhile, Nell leaned out the tree house window. Aside from lots of branches and leaves, there wasn't much to see. Was it possible that the ghost had been real? But then, out of the corner of her eye . . . "Detective Doyle, wait, I think I see something!"

Quick as a wink, Drake popped his head out of the other window.

"There!" Nell pointed. "Looks like some kind of pipe is caught in a branch."

Drake pushed up his glasses. "It's PVC pipe."

"And there's something bright orange on the end of it," said Nell.

"Why would PVC pipe be in a tree?" asked Drake. "It's used for plumbing."

"Excellent question, Detective Doyle. Let's knock it out of the tree and see if it holds any clues."

As they were roping off the backyard with yellow tape, they noticed a long, thin board propped against Valerie's house. And even though there was a nail head poking out the top end of the board, it came in quite handy. Drake used the board to knock the PVC pipe out of the tree and onto the ground.

Immediately they fetched some surgical gloves from their backpacks and put them on. (Amateur scientist detective geniuses can never be too careful while handling clues.)

Snap!

Snap!

Nell picked up the pipe. "Curious. Someone has cut the neck off of a balloon to make a round piece of rubber and then stretched it over the end of the PVC pipe—"

"Securing it with a rubber band," added Drake.

"Other than that," said Nell, "the pipe is empty."

They took a few moments to jot their discovery into their lab notebooks.

Then, just as they were about to continue their investigation, Drake tripped and fell *splat!* on his face. "Oh dear," he said. But unlike most other times Drake had fallen, this time it was a stroke of luck. You see, Drake's face just happened to fall right on another clue. Another balloon, to be precise.

"Good work, Detective Doyle." Nell helped him up and brushed him off. She examined the clue. "Hmm. The balloon appears to be cut in the same way. Except there's a small hole in the center of this one." Nell looked at Drake. "Do you suppose it was wrapped around the other end of the PVC pipe?"

Drake wiped off his glasses and slipped them on. "It is the most logical explanation. But *why* is the question."

Nell scratched her head, stumped. "Why indeed, Detective Doyle. We need more clues."

Searching the area on their hands and knees, they found a brown paper bag with the words MOSSY LAKE ICE & FUEL stamped on the outside.

Just then, Nell had a feeling. (It's a feeling all scientists get when they think they're on the right track, but don't precisely know why. Commonly known as a hunch.) Without another word, she walked up to Valerie's house and rapped on the door.

Valerie opened the door a crack. "Did you, like, find the ghost already? Is the case solved? Can you, like, totally get off my property now?"

"Tell me, Ms. Applegate," said Nell. "Who was at your slumber party last night?"

"I mean, there was . . ." and she listed about five names. "And, I *was*, like, gonna invite Sloane Westcott, but she said my perm totally looked like poodle fuzz, so I said, like, forget *her*."

Nell cocked her eyebrow. "Interesting. You don't happen to have a photograph of Sloane, do you?"

Valerie rolled her eyes, chomped her gum, and sighed. "I suppose. Wait here a sec."

While Valerie left to fetch a photo of Sloane, Nell said, "Something smells fishy."

Drake nodded. "Things having to do with Sloane usually smell fishy."

You see, they'd had cases involving Sloane before. In fact, one case had involved, of all things, a ghost. Of course, it hadn't really been a ghost at all, just a scheme between Sloane and Frisco to make some money. And Doyle and Fossey had busted their scheme.

After a moment Valerie reappeared with a photo. She handed it to Nell. "We took it at our last party."

It was a photo of the Snob Club. Nell put it in her lab-coat pocket. "We'll return it when we're finished, Ms. Applegate. We'll call as soon as we know anything."

Back at the bikes, Nell placed the PVC pipe, the balloons, and the paper bag in her bicycle basket. "So, Detective Doyle. Now that we think we know whodunit, the question is, *how* did she do it?"

"There's only one way to find out, Scientist Nell," said Drake, climbing onto his bike.

"Indeed. To Mossy Lake Ice & Fuel."

CHAPTER SEVEN

Ghost Busting

Mossy Lake Ice & Fuel was up a ways, a little to the right, and down a couple more streets. They parked their bikes, marched inside, and handed their business card to the man behind the counter.

"Doyle and Fossey, Science Detectives," said Drake.

The man peered at the card. "And I'm Bill Watson. What can I get for you two? Ice? Fuel?"

"Information," replied Nell. She handed Mr. Watson the photo and pointed to Sloane. "Have you seen her?"

"She was here yesterday." He handed back the photo. "Rudest girl I ever met. Called me a bonehead, with a brain no bigger than the ear wax of a pickle."

Nell glanced at Drake. "Sounds like Sloane, all right." (Sloane was, by far, the rudest girl in the entire fifth grade. Perhaps even the rudest girl *ever*, fifth grade or otherwise.)

Drake asked, "And what was she doing here?"

"She bought some ice."

Drake cocked his eyebrow. "Let me guess. Was it dry ice?"

The man nodded. "Bought a whole bunch of it, too."

Nell and Drake glanced at each other. This was the break they'd been looking for.

Nell shook Mr. Watson's hand. "Thanks. You've been a great help."

Outside, they climbed on their bikes.

"To the lab," said Nell. "For analysis."

"Check," said Drake. "We have a ghost to bust."

Back at the lab, Nell pulled a book off the shelf. She found the section titled: "Ghosts in the Tree House: What to Do When You're Having a Slumber Party, Your Hair Looks Like Poodle Fuzz, and a Ghost Breathes on the Back of Your Neck." After she read aloud, she and Drake discussed all of their clues.

Then they developed a plan. A ghostly plan. A ghostly ghost-busting plan.

Nell called Valerie. "Ms. Applegate? Nell Fossey here. We're on the verge of a breakthrough, but we need your help. . . ."

That night, Nell took cover behind a bush in Valerie's backyard. The moon was full, and the stars twinkled nicely. (The perfect sort of night for busting ghosts.) Across the backyard and on the other side of the tree house, Drake also hid behind a bush.

Nell spoke into her walkie-talkie. "Coffee Nut to Muffin Man. Coffee Nut to Muffin Man. Come in. Over."

"Muffin Man here," replied Drake's voice. "Over."

"I'm in position. Over."

"Roger that. I'm in position, too. Over."

"Roger that, Muffin Man. Let me know if you see anything. Over."

"Copy that, Coffee Nut. Over and out."

And so they waited. And waited.

Meanwhile, Nell heard giggles coming from the tree house. As Nell had requested, Valerie had organized another slumber party and invited every snob except Sloane. If all went according to plan, then . . .

Suddenly, a twig snapped. Someone was out there!

"Muffin Man, come in," Nell whispered into the walkie-talkie. "Did you hear that?"

"Loud and clear, Coffee Nut. Our ghost has arrived."

Nell peered through the bush. Sure enough, Sloane stood under the tree. She fiddled a few moments with something, put it on the end of the long board, and then raised the board high above her head and into the tree.

There was a rustle of leaves.

A scream. (According to plan.) "The ghost! Aaahh! The ghost!"

Nell said into the walkie-talkie, "Now, Muffin Man, now!"

"Roger that, Coffee Nut!"

And out they pounced, shining their flashlights into Sloane's surprised face.

"Drop it!" they cried. "Hands in the air! You're busted!"

The PVC pipe clattered to the ground as Sloane dropped the board. She put her hands on her hips and glared at Drake and Nell. "I should've known you two would mess up my brilliant scheme of terrifying revenge. Don't you beaker brains ever get any sleep? And quit shining that thing in my face, will you?"

Drake ignored her and spoke into his walkie-talkie, "Muffin Man to Snob Club. Muffin Man to Snob Club. Come in, Snob Club."

"Snob Club here," came Valerie's voice.

"Ghost apprehended. Over."

It took a few moments for Valerie and her friends to climb down from the tree house. Of course, they weren't surprised to see Sloane. "Drake and Nell, like, told us it was you," said Valerie.

"Get lost, poodle puff," said Sloane.

Drake put himself in between them. "Now, now. Let's be civilized and get on with it, shall we? I'm sure you're all wondering exactly what Sloane was doing, and how we cracked the case."

"Not really," said Sloane.

Drake ignored her. "It was quite simple, once we had all our clues. Allow Scientist Nell to explain."

"Thank you, Detective Doyle." Nell clasped her hands behind her back and began to pace. "Now, any good scientist will tell you that 'matter' is defined as anything that has weight and takes up space. For instance, the planet Earth is composed of matter. This tree is composed of matter. You, Sloane, are made of matter."

"And there's plenty the matter with you, too," snapped Sloane.

"Be quiet, Sloane," said Valerie. "You are, like, so busted."

Sloane scowled and crossed her arms.

"Now," continued Nell, "matter can exist as a solid, a liquid, or a gas. Water is a perfect example of the three phases of matter. When frozen, it is a solid. At room temperature, it is a liquid. Boil water, and you see it rising as steam, or gas."

"Well said," said Drake.

"But *dry ice* is a different matter altogether," said Nell. "You see, dry ice is composed of carbon dioxide—"

"Frozen to a temperature of minus one hundred and nine degrees Fahrenheit," said Drake. "Only, when dry ice melts it doesn't turn into a liquid. It goes directly from a solid to a gas."

"It's called sublimation," said Nell.

"But, like, what does dry ice have to do with the ghost?" asked Valerie, chomping her gum. "I mean, like, we haven't even done our nails yet, and it's getting kinda late."

"Excellent question, Ms. Applegate," said Drake. "Simply put, Sloane put dry ice into this PVC pipe, covered both ends with balloons, and then added water through the little hole in one of the balloons."

"The dry ice melted rapidly in the water—" said Nell.

"But," added Drake, "it melted into a *gas*. A *cold* gas, I might add, which then shot out through the hole in the balloon and froze your neck."

"Allow me to demonstrate," said Nell. And without further ado, she whipped out a ready-made demonstration kit from behind the bush. Both Nell and Drake pulled on heavy gloves and put on their safety glasses. And while everyone watched, Nell poured water into a bowl. In the bowl was a chunk of dry ice. Vapor instantly rose from the dry ice, looking quite spooky.

"You see," said Drake, "Sloane attached the pipe to the end of this long board using a nail and a rubber band. She loaded the pipe with dry-ice chips and a few drops of water and then hoisted the board through the branches. When the dry-ice blaster was high enough, she aimed it through the cracks in the tree house. Purely diabolical."

"Diabolical, indeed," said Nell.

Valerie turned to Sloane. "You are, like, so out of the Snob Club."

"Spare me the gory details," said Sloane. "Oh, wait . . . I think I'm gonna cry. Wait . . . wait . . . here it comes . . . no . . . guess not. Better luck next time, poodle puff." And with a purely diabolical laugh, Sloane stalked off into the shadows.

Drake handed Valerie their business card. "Call us, anytime."

"Like, you know, thanks a bunch," said Valerie. "I'll totally give you a free weekend in the tree house as payment, man. Just don't touch anything."

"All in a night's work." Nell shook Valerie's hand, once again satisfied with a job well done.

And off went Drake and Nell into the night, another ghost busted.

CHAPTER EIGHT
The Pits

Drake snapped the rubber band into place. Then he turned the crank, which turned a wheel, which whirled the blades. A breeze began to blow. "Ahh," he sighed, dabbing his brow with a hankie.

He scribbled in his lab notebook:

New invention quite cool.
Just the thing for a hot day.

As Drake shut his notebook, the phone rang.

"Doyle and Fossey," Drake answered, sounding quite cool and collected.

"Mighty glad you're there, Drake Doyle." Drake recognized the drawl. It was Jessie Simmons, the new girl in class. Just last week, her family had moved from Oklahoma to Mossy Lake. Jessie wore a cowgirl hat and boots, said things like "Ain't life grand?" and twirled her lasso during recess.

"What can I do for you today, Ms. Simmons?" Drake replied.

"Something plumb awful's happened. My poor little pet pig, Dolly, broke out of her pigpen and fell into a pit."

Drake breathed a sigh of relief. Rescuing a piglet sounded like easy work. Easy work was a good thing on such a hot, hot day.

"You gotta come quick," Jessie was saying.

"'Quick' is our middle name. Exactly where do you live, Ms. Simmons?"

"The ranch house at Porcupine Loop. Hurry!"

Immediately Drake phoned Nell. "Piglet meets pit at Porcupine Poop—I—I mean, Porcupine Loop. Meet me at the ranch house."

"Check."

Click.

Naturally, Nell was already there by the time Drake rode up. (Not only was she the fastest runner in the fifth grade, but she could ride like the wind, too.) She stood waiting for him with her notebook in hand, a pencil behind each ear, and Dr. Livingston at her side. Nell was about the handiest partner a science detective genius could ask for. "Ready?" she asked.

"Ready," said Drake.

Just then, Jessie came running around the side of the house. Her pigtails were messy, and dirt was smeared across her face. "Thank the stars, you're here! Follow me 'round back. Hurry! Poor little Dolly's in the pit."

They followed Jessie. She ran behind the house and then pointed down. There, in the ground, was a very dark opening to a very dark pit.

"It's an old, dried-out well," Jessie explained. "Dad was going to fill it in next week once we got settled. He put a piece of plywood over it so no one would fall in."

Drake pushed up his glasses. "How did Dolly fall in, if it was covered with plywood?"

"See for yourselves," said Jessie, still pointing.

Drake whipped out his flashlight and flicked it on. Together, Drake, Nell, and Jessie peered down the well. "Helloooooo, Dolly!" cried Drake.

Down, down, down, went the well.

Helloooooo, Dolly! went the echo.

And then they saw her. It was horrible. It was awful. Quite possibly, it was their worst nightmare, ever. You see, Dolly wasn't a little piglet at all. Dolly was ONE BIG FAT PIG! In fact, she looked more like a baby hippo than a baby pig.

OINK! oinked Dolly.

"Great Scott!" cried Drake.

Woof! yelped Dr. Livingston.

"She's enormous!" cried Nell. "She broke right through the plywood!"

"This is impossible!" cried Drake. "We'll never get her out!"

And then, as if finding one big fat pig at the bottom of a deep dark well on a hot, hot day wasn't bad enough, Jessie burst into tears. That's right. She sat back on her cowgirl boots and just blubbered. It was pitiful.

Drake and Nell looked at each other, astonished. Other than watching Jessie twirl her lasso at school, they really didn't know her very well. "Uh, anything we can do for you, Ms. Simmons?" asked Drake. "Hankie, perhaps?"

Jessie wiped her nose on her sleeve. "Goshdurnit, Drake, Dolly's my best friend. She's the only thing I got to take with me from Oklahoma. All my other critters done got sold. If Dolly's a goner, I think the twirl will go right out of my lasso. I'm plumb lost without her."

"Can't your parents help?" asked Nell.

"They're in Oklahoma, attending the Poultry Producers' Prancing Promenade. My grandma's the only one here. And she can't lift Dolly."

"Fire department?" asked Drake.

"I already tried them. They said they'd be right over, 'cause they ain't had a pork barbecue for about a week now and they was starved. 'Course I told them thank you kindly, but never mind. Don't you see? You just *gotta* save Dolly."

"Well," said Drake. "Looks like it's up to us."

"But what can we do?" asked Nell. "We can't just lasso her and pull her up. She must weigh one hundred eighty pounds."

"Two hundred," corrected Jessie.

Both Drake and Nell gasped. Drake crunched a few numbers with his calculator. Meanwhile, Nell glanced around, searching for something to help them. There were a few things—a shovel, a tarp, an old rusty swing set—but not much.

"We must return to the lab," said Drake.

"Agreed," said Nell.

"We'll be back in an hour," said Drake.

"Please hurry," said Jessie, wiping away a tear. "My heart's about broke."

So off they rode, with Dr. Livingston racing ahead.

CHAPTER NINE

A Foolproof Plan

As Jessie watched Drake and Nell ride away, the little lump in her throat became a big lump.

"Don't you worry none, Dolly," cried Jessie into the pit. "Doyle and Fossey, Science Detectives, are gonna save you . . . at least I think they are." She suddenly realized she didn't know much about Doyle and Fossey. Maybe they could save Dolly, but maybe they *couldn't*. Maybe . . . maybe . . .

Jessie dug in her pocket and pulled out another business card. "Frisco," the card read. She'd been warned that his prices were steep and that he wasn't nearly so polite as Doyle and Fossey. But if he could save Dolly . . .

Jessie ran into the house to make a quick phone call.

Meanwhile, back at the lab, Drake and Nell had already read the section in their handy reference book titled: "Porker Problems: What to Do When a Big Fat Pig Has Fallen into a Pit and Can't Get Out."

"We need to formulate a plan," said Drake, pushing his glasses up.

"A foolproof plan." Nell took a quick gulp of decaf. "Because if it fails . . . well, the possibilities are just too horrible to imagine."

"Here's what I think we should do," said Drake, and they put their heads together and formulated a foolproof plan.

After gathering all the necessary equipment, they set out again, pedaling like mad. (With Nell's decaf in a to-go mug.) But when they arrived in Jessie's backyard, what they saw was shocking beyond words.

They saw Frisco and Baloney tugging on a rope that led out of the pit.

"Ugh!"

"Grunt!"

OINK!

Now, in case you didn't know, Baloney was Frisco's best friend and easily the biggest kid at

Seaview Elementary School. If anyone could pull one big fat pig from a pit, it was Baloney. Drake knew from experience just how big Baloney was, as he often sat on Drake if Drake came too close or if Baloney just happened to feel like sitting on something. (Having Baloney sit on you was rather like having a refrigerator sit on you, or a rhinoceros.)

Drake was so shocked that he dropped his armload of equipment with a clatter. "Great Scott!"

Nell dropped her decaf. "Oh my gosh!"

Woof! said Dr. Livingston.

"Hey, look who's here," said Baloney, stopping for a breather. "It's those other guys."

Nell put her hands on her hips. "Better known as Doyle and Fossey, Science Detectives."

Frisco frowned. "What're *you* doing here?"

"We were hired by Ms. Simmons to handle this most difficult case," said Drake.

"Oh yeah?" said Frisco. "Well, so was I. And I was here first, so beat it, brainiacs."

Jessie broke in between them. "Y'all, please. It's my fault, I reckon. You see, I hired all y'all. I—I just want someone to save Dolly. It don't matter who. Please don't make a fuss. Please save her. *Please.*"

Frisco snorted. "Well, so long as they stay out of our way and let us men do our job." And he and Baloney went back to pulling on their rope.

"Ugh!"

"Grunt!"

OINK!

Nell murmured to Drake. "Jessie must have lassoed Dolly for them. At this rate, not only will it take them all day, but Dolly will still be in the pit by the end of it and very sore, besides."

"Agreed," said Drake. "They're going about it all wrong."

"Shall we?" asked Nell.

"Indeed," replied Drake. "Let's get to work."

And so they did.

With Jessie's help, they moved the old rusty swing set into position. They suspended ropes. They hung pulleys. They tied knots. They scratched Dr. Livingston behind his ears.

Finally, Jessie climbed a rope ladder down into the pit and attached a harness to Dolly. Then Jessie climbed back up. (But not before she gave Dolly a few hugs and whispered some sweet nothin's.)

"Ready," she said.

"All systems go!" cried Drake.

"Stand back, Frisco and Baloney," cried Nell, "and let the *real* scientists do their work!"

And with some gentle tugging, Drake and Nell drew in the rope a foot at a time, while the pulleys turned. It was easy work, really. They scarcely broke a sweat. And Dolly rose up out of the pit, lickety-split. *Oink!*

"Hey!" cried Frisco and Baloney. "No fair!"

Then, with a quick lasso from Jessie, Dolly was hauled to the side and released. "Oh, Dolly!" Jessie wrapped her arms around Dolly.

Oink! oinked Dolly, wagging her little piggy tail.

It was quite a tender moment, really. (Drake dabbed his eyes with a hankie.)

Jessie said, "You done saved my little pig's life, Drake and Nell. How were you able to do it when Frisco and Baloney couldn't?"

"Simple," said Frisco, scowling. "They were cheating."

Drake adjusted his glasses. "Frisco is right. It was simple. But it wasn't cheating. Allow Scientist Nell to explain."

"Thank you, Detective Doyle. To begin with, moving a pig out of a pit requires a lot of work."

"Tell me about it," mumbled Baloney.

"However, simple machines help make work simple," said Nell.

"Hence the name 'simple machines,'" added Drake.

Nell continued, "With the help of simple machines—pulleys in this case—Detective Doyle and I were able to do the work using less force. You see, pulleys are like miniature wheels."

"Quite handy, really," said Drake.

"The first thing pulleys can do for us is change the direction of the force." Nell drew a quick sketch in her notebook. "Instead of having to pull a load *upward*, one pulley and a rope can let you pull *downward*."

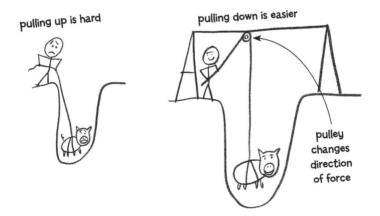

pulling up is hard

pulling down is easier

pulley changes direction of force

"Which," mentioned Drake, "makes the work easier."

"Blah, blah," said Frisco. "Easier, schmeasier."

"The second thing pulleys do for us," said Drake, "is divide the load, again making the work easier. Scientist Nell?"

"Thank you, Detective Doyle. You see, *work* is defined as the *force,* or weight of an object, multiplied by the *distance* to be moved. In our case, we had to lift a two-hundred-pound pig out of a twenty-foot pit."

"But by using a multiple pulley system—" said Drake.

"Dolly's weight, or force, was divided between each of the pulleys." Nell drew another sketch. "Now, let's say, instead of pulling a rope with a force of two hundred pounds, we pull a rope with a force of, say, fifty pounds, or twenty. It just depends on how many pulleys we use."

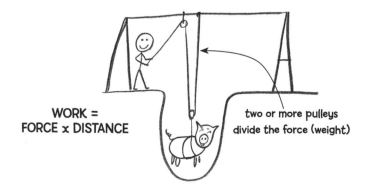

WORK =
FORCE x DISTANCE

two or more pulleys
divide the force (weight)

"All we have to do is pull more rope," added Drake.

"Again, far easier. Force is traded for distance," said Nell. "It takes more rope and a little more time to set up, but it's not nearly so hard."

"Simple, if I do say so myself," remarked Drake.

"I just can't thank y'all enough," said Jessie. "Doyle and Fossey, you're everything everyone said you'd be."

"Hey, what about me?" asked Frisco.

Jessie scuffed the dirt with her cowgirl boot. "Well, you're everything everyone said you'd be, too, I reckon."

Nell handed her their business card. "Call us. Anytime."

Back in the lab once again, Drake wrote in his lab notebook:

For a hard day's work, it was a snap.
Jessie and Dolly reunited at last.
Received free lasso lessons.
Paid in full.

70

Activities and Experiments for Super-Scientists

Contents

Your Own Lab

Every good scientist needs a laboratory. It's quite simple, really. All you need is a work space, like a desk or a card table. Add a lamp, stir in some supplies, stick a pencil behind your ear, and presto! Here are some tips for creating your own lab:

1. Start out by collecting some odds and ends, such as glass bottles, jars, string, balloons, a magnifying glass, or rubber bands. You never know when these might come in handy. Safety glasses are a must for any well-stocked lab.

2. Of course, every good scientist keeps a lab notebook. A spiral notebook is perfect. Record everything, such as: hypothesis, procedure, observations, results, and conclusions. (Don't forget to record your mistakes, too!)

3. No top-notch scientist would feel quite right without a lab coat. Make your own lab coat by using an old button-down shirt. (Ask first!)

Write your name on it with a permanent marker.

4. Keep masking tape and a marker handy for labeling. All good scientists label what they are working on so they won't mix things up.

5. Sometimes real scientists are exposed to dangerous chemicals or harmful bacteria. Good scientists can reduce the risk of exposure by wearing protective gear and by washing their hands frequently. What does this mean for you? Wear safety glasses or gloves if required. Wash your hands and clean up your work space when you are finished with an experiment. Never put your hands near your eyes or mouth until after you have washed them with soap and water. If you're unsure about anything, ask an adult.

Yakkity-Yak

Scientists from all over the world talk with one another. They hold conferences and publish their findings in scientific journals. In a way, no matter what country they're from, scientists speak the same language. They all use the scientific method.

Drake and Nell do, too. (Frisco doesn't.) Drake and Nell observe carefully, and jot their observations in their lab notebooks. (Frisco, however, doesn't even own a lab notebook. Or a sharpened pencil.) Based upon their observations, Drake and Nell then develop a hypothesis, as they did in Chapter Three. A hypothesis is a scientist's best guess as to what is happening and why. (Frisco, on the other hand, plugs his ears and hums loudly whenever anyone mentions a hypothesis.)

The barfy birthday hypothesis might have sounded something like this: *Based upon our observations, we believe something at the birthday party made people barf.* Like all good scientists, Drake and Nell tested their hypothesis. In this case, they called everyone who'd attended the party and asked questions about what they did, what they ate, etc.

Did you know?
In 1976, over 200 people became mysteriously ill while attending an American Legion Convention in a Philadelphia hotel. Epidemiologists sprang into action. They investigated everything: the food, the rest rooms, the water, you name it. The culprit? The water in the air-conditioning system was loaded with deadly bacteria. People became sick just by breathing the cooled air. The new disease was named *Legionnaires' disease.*

Brainteasers for Bacteria Busters

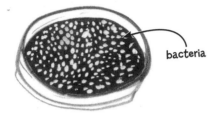

bacteria

Imagine it. Mossy Lake. Present day. Everything is peachy until, suddenly, *choke! gasp! barf!* . . half the town becomes sick. And not just sick, but *sick* sick.

Enter the bacteria busters. Known in the scientific world as epidemiologists. (Rather like ghost busters, except they walk around in lab coats, carry clipboards, and ask lots of questions.)

Their job? To find out what is making some people sick but not others. In other words, to find the common factor, or source, and then to take steps to keep the sickness from spreading. Drake and Nell found the common factor in the Case of the Barfy Birthday. It was the chicken salad.

Here's part of their master chart:

Name	Are they sick?	Ate cake	Swung at piñata	Ate chicken salad	Took a dip in the pool	Drank punch	Ate a hamburger
Zoe		y	y	N	y	N	y
Chloe		y	y	y	y	y	N
Mrs. Jackson		N	N	y	y	N	y
Lilly Crump		y	N	y	N	y	y
Drake		y	y	N	y	N	N
Nell		N	y	N	y	y	N
Baloney		y (3 helpings)	y	y (2 helpings)	y	y (8 glasses)	y (6 burgers)

Enter you—Bacteria Buster. Your mission is to bend your brain around the following questions. Grab a clipboard, paper, and pencil. Copy down the chart. Scratch your head. Jot down notes. Whatever you do, don't give up. The town depends upon you. For each question, start over again using the original chart:

1. Suppose that:
    (1) Chloe, Lilly, Nell, and Baloney are sick, and
    (2) Zoe, Mrs. Jackson, and Drake are not sick.
    What is the common factor?

2. Suppose that:

(1) Zoe, Mrs. Jackson, Lilly, and Baloney are sick, and

(2) Chloe, Drake, and Nell are not sick.

Now what is the common factor?

3. What if:

(1) Zoe, Chloe, and Baloney are sick, and

(2) Mrs. Jackson, Lilly, Drake, and Nell are not sick

AND . . .

(3) Everyone ate cake.

(4) Everyone swung at the piñata.

(5) No one ate chicken salad.

(6) Everyone took a dip in the pool.

(7) Everyone drank punch.

(8) Everyone ate a hamburger except Nell, because she's a vegetarian.

Now what is the common factor?

Answers: (1) Punch (2) Hamburger (3) None of them. Why? Because Mrs. Jackson, Lilly, and Drake did everything, too, and yet they aren't sick at all. (And if no one ate the chicken salad, it couldn't possibly be the culprit.) At this point an epidemiologist must scratch his head and keep looking. Maybe there is a question that has not been asked—such as, were there other foods or drinks? Other activities? Was there someplace else besides the party where people could have gotten sick, such as school? You see, an epidemiologist must also be a detective.

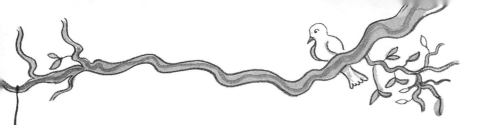

Be a Bird Buddy

Like many wild animals, birds are losing their wild habitats at a fast pace. You can learn more about birds and even help them by becoming a bird buddy. Here are some tips:

1. What kinds of birds live where you do?
   • Check out a bird-identification book from your local library or use one of these on-line bird books:
      • www.allaboutbirds.org
      • www.enature.com (Complete with birdsongs!)
      • http://www.birdwatchersdigest.com/site/backyard_birds/bird_id/species_index.aspx
   • You'll need a pair of binoculars, a lab notebook, and colored pencils. Make a table of your bird sightings. It could look something like this:

Species Name	Picture	Date	How many?	Where?	Endangered?
American Robin			18	In my backyard	No
Stellar's Jay			2	By Mossy Lake	No

2. Create a bird-friendly backyard:
   • Build a bird feeder: Mix ¼ cup creamy peanut butter with ¼ cup cornmeal. Smear the mixture over a pinecone with a butter knife, then roll the pinecone in birdseed. Use a piece of string to hang the pinecone from a tree branch. Recoat the pinecone as needed.
   • Provide plenty of shrubs, trees, or nesting boxes for birds to nest in.

3. If you find a baby bird, leave it alone. Many baby birds leave the nest before they are ready to fly. This is natural. The parent is almost always nearby, protecting it and feeding it until the chick finds its wings.

4. For more information on birds and backyard birding, check out these bird-buddy Web sites:
   - www.birding.com
   - www.wildbirds.com
   - www.birdwatching.com
   - www.birdwatchersdigest.com

Did you know?

As the human population grows, it needs more land to survive. Every day a natural habitat as large as New York City is being harvested, turned into farmland, or developed for housing. Habitat destruction is the leading cause of extinction. Extinction occurs when a species of plant or animal, such as a jaguar, no longer exists. Extinction is forever. Today, animal and plant species are becoming extinct at a greater rate than ever before. Scientists say that 137 species become extinct *every day*.

How Can I Help?

"Take nothing but pictures . . . leave nothing but footsteps" is good advice when visiting a wild habitat. Don't pick any wildflowers or berries, and don't take anything that you didn't bring with you in the first place. Stay on the trail provided.

When watching wildlife, only watch. Stay a safe distance away and respect their territory.

Don't litter. Trash looks terrible and can harm wildlife. Six-pack plastic soda rings can strangle wildlife. (Snip the rings apart, including the center.) Also, don't release balloons into the air, as sea turtles and seabirds could mistake them for food and then choke.

When a species is "endangered," it is on the brink of extinction. Check out this Web site to learn more about endangered species and how you can help protect wildlife habitats:

http://www.nrdc.org/reference/kids.asp

Send a Secret Message

Y4X4. Y4X3. Y4X2. Y5X6.
Y3X1. Y4X3
Y3X6. Y3X5. Y2X1.

What was that gibberish that Nell sent to Drake? Martian? Plutonian? It's quite simple, once you crack the code. Here's the code breaking grid Drake and Nell used:

(You can put the letters of the alphabet wherever you want.) Using the grid to the right, if you want to write the letter **J**—first find

y5	H	P	Y	K	A	D
y4	G	S	E	F	C	U
y3	M	T	A	E	O	N
y2	W	R	J	B	I	E
y1	Q	I	X	Z	L	V
	X1	X2	X3	X4	X5	X6

which **Y** row contains **J**, then which **X** column. **J** is found at **Y2** and **X3**. To make it harder for your enemies to read, put the **Y** and **X** numbers together: **Y2X3**. Here are some other examples:

Z = Y1X4   O = Y3X5   E = Y4X3   ZOE = Y1X4.Y3X5.Y4X3

To practice, decipher the following message:

Y4X2.Y4X6.Y5X2.Y3X4.Y2X2

Y4X2.Y4X5.Y2X5.Y4X3.Y3X6.Y3X2.Y1X2.Y4X2.Y3X2.Y4X2

Y2X2.Y3X5.Y4X5.Y5X4

Answer: Super-Scientists Rock

83

Dry-Ice Blaster

Imagine it. You're the frozen dead. Fresh from the grave—the frozen grave . . .

Or you're just hot and need to cool off.

Anyway, here's how to build your own dry-ice blaster, just like Sloane did to scare the Snob Club.

MATERIALS

- heavy gloves
- safety glasses
- 5 lbs. dry ice cut into 1-lb. pieces (See box on page 87 for dry-ice safety info)
- newspaper
- hammer
- scissors
- 2 large balloons
- PVC pipe, at least 10" long, with about 1½" diameter (dimensions not critical)
- rubber bands

- tablespoon
- funnel
- measuring cup
- water
- plastic or Styrofoam cooler

PROCEDURE

1. Read and follow the notes on dry-ice safety with an adult. Don't be a Frisco!

2. Put on heavy gloves and safety glasses.

3. Fold 1 pound of dry ice into a newspaper and pound with a hammer until the dry ice is a powder. (Best done outdoors on a sidewalk.)

4. Cut the necks off 2 balloons.

5. Stretch 1 balloon over one end of the PVC pipe. Secure with a rubber band.

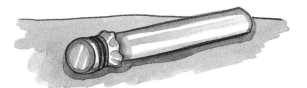

6. Add 5 spoonfuls of dry-ice powder into the PVC pipe. The balloon will keep the powder from falling out the bottom.

7. Poke a hole in the center of the second balloon. The hole should be just big enough to squeeze the end of the funnel through it.

8. As in step #5, stretch the balloon over the other end of the PVC pipe and secure with a rubber band. Hole should be in the center of the pipe's opening.

9. Place funnel in hole.

10. Quickly pour ¼ cup water into the funnel.

11. Remove funnel and blast away. (**Never** point the blaster at anyone's face.)

12. When the volume of gas dies down, shaking the pipe can help revive it. Add more water if it helps. At some point, you will need to undo the top balloon and start over with fresh-crushed dry ice.

13. Store extra dry ice in a cooler until you need it.

Dry-Ice Information and Safety:

Adult supervision required! Dry ice, when properly handled, can be loads of fun. But when not used safely, dry ice can cause injury.

• Always wear heavy gloves when handling dry ice—it can cause frostbite if you touch it with your bare skin. Wear safety glasses to protect your eyes from possible flying ice chips!

• Look in your local Yellow Pages under "Dry Ice" for places that sell it. They will cut the dry ice for you.

• Place dry ice in a plastic or Styrofoam cooler while transporting it. Store dry ice in your cooler rather than in your freezer. It will last about 24 hours.

• Carbon-dioxide gas is heavy and can become concentrated in enclosed spaces. It can eventually replace the oxygen in a room or car, causing asphyxiation. Always leave a window cracked to allow air to flow freely throughout the room or vehicle.

• Try not to breathe carbon-dioxide fumes. Remember, it replaces the oxygen your body needs.

• Never taste or swallow dry ice.

• Protect your tabletops and countertops from dry ice by using newspaper or towels. The extreme cold could cause the countertop to crack.

• Dispose of dry ice by putting it outside in a well-ventilated container, away from small children and animals.

Other Super-Scientific Stuff

So . . . you're the frozen dead sitting there with dry ice and balloons. What to do now? Try this: Place a funnel in the neck of a balloon and add a few spoonfuls of dry-ice powder. Tie the neck of the balloon. Stand back. Watch the balloon expand and then explode! (Do outdoors, far away from anything that might not like being exploded on.)

Try this, too (great for spooky parties): In a well-ventilated room or outside, put a chunk of dry ice in a large bowl of water and see what happens.

Trouble in the Tree House

The Scene: You and your friend have built a magnificent tree house. The biggest one in the neighborhood. The highest one for miles around. The most comfy.

The Problem: Now that you're snug in your tree house, you and your friend realize you're both very, very hungry.

You scramble down the ladder, shimmy down the wood blocks hammered into the tree trunk, and finally slide down the dangling rope until you reach the ground. Ahh, you think, *food*. And you load up for the trip back. (You know—cookies, cheese, sandwiches, pop, chips, etc.)

But at the base of the tree, you stop short. Uh-oh. A terrible question comes to mind. How do you get food to your tree house when you have to climb using both your hands? You know you can't use a backpack to carry all your food, because you will then be too heavy to pull yourself up the rope. After all, remember, you're *very,*

very hungry and feeling a little weak. (Besides, what about that TV set that's next on your list of tree house musts?)

Stumped? Try the following activity for a clue on how to make the work simple.

MATERIALS

- tape
- paper cup
- paper clip
- handful of small rocks
- string
- scissors
- 2 pulleys (available in hardware stores)

PROCEDURE

1. Cut a short piece of string and tape it securely to the top of the paper cup. This is your handle.

2. Put a handful of rocks into the cup.

3. Using another short piece of string, tie

one of the pulleys to the back of a chair so that it hangs freely. This is pulley **A**.

4. Cut a piece of string three times as long as the height of the chair. For example, if the height of the chair is 4 feet, cut a piece of string 12 feet long [3 x 4 = 12].

5. Tie one end of the piece of string to the back of the chair. Thread the string through the second pulley (pulley **B**) and then through pulley **A**.

6. Secure the other end of the string by tying it to another piece of furniture so that your system remains tight and does not collapse.

7. Using the paper clip as a hook, attach the cup full of rocks to pulley **B**.

8. Untie the end of the string from the piece of furniture (see step #6). Pull string down to lift cup.

9. Up, down. Up, down. Snack time!

How Does This Work?

Pulley A changes the direction of the force. Instead of having to lift the cup up, you can now relax on the couch and pull the string down, with the same effect.

Using two or more pulleys divides the load. In this setup, if your rock-filled cup weighs 1 pound, pulley B reduces the weight (or force) you must pull by one-half. Now, instead of pulling 1 pound of rocks, you are pulling ½ pound. In return, you must pull twice the length of string. As a test, try the same setup *without* pulley B. Feel and see the difference?